Nate the Great
and The

STOLEN BASE

Nate the Great
and The
STOLEN BASE

WITHDRAWN

by Marjorie Weinman Sharmat

illustrations by Marc Simont

A YEARLING BOOK

Published by Yearling, an imprint of Random House Children's Books
a division of Random House, Inc., New York

Visit us on the Web! www.randomhouse.com/kids

Educators and librarians, for a variety of teaching tools,
visit us at www.randomhouse.com/teachers

ISBN-13: 978-0-440-40932-8
ISBN-10: 0-440-40932-2

Reprinted by arrangement with The Putnam Publishing Group Inc.
Printed in the United States of America
One Previous Edition
New Yearling Edition May 2006
45 44 43 42
UPR

For my father, Nathan "Nate" Weinman,
and with appreciation to all the Nathans everywhere
who feel a special bond with Nate the Great

I, Nate the Great, am a detective.
Sometimes I'm a baseball player.
This morning I was a detective
and a baseball player.
My dog, Sludge, and I
went to the field.
I had to practice batting
and running and fielding.
I belong to a team.

ROSAMOND'S RANGERS.

Rosamond, Annie, Harry,

Oliver, Esmeralda, Claude,

Finley, and Pip belong too.

They were at the field.

Rosamond's four cats were there.

They are the team's mascots.

Annie's dog Fang was there.

Fang is not on the team.

He is not a mascot.

Fang should have stayed home.

Rosamond came up to me.

"We can't practice today," she said.

"Somebody stole second base."

"We can get another second base,"

I said. I bent down

and picked up a big stone.

"A stone for second base?"

Rosamond said.

"Not while I'm coach.

Everybody uses stones.

Rosamond's Rangers do not."

Rosamond is a strange coach.

That was no surprise.

Rosamond is a strange person.

She said, "When we play

baseball, I bring first base.

Oliver brings second base.

And Annie brings third base."

Rosamond held up a

large tuna fish can.

"Here's today's first base.

Nobody stole it."

Annie held up a large dog bone.

"Here's today's third base," she said.

"Nobody ate it."

Fang and Sludge sniffed.

Oliver said,

"I was going to bring

the same base I brought yesterday.

But somebody stole it.

It was the best."

I, Nate the Great, did not think

Oliver's second base was the best.

It was an octopus

made of gloopy purple plastic.

Oliver collects eels.

He is saving up

for a real octopus.

"We need a detective to find

my second base," he said.

"Make another octopus," I said.

Oliver was mad.

"You think it's easy to make

those long, curling arms?" he said.

"Besides, that was

my good-luck octopus."

"Very well. I, Nate the Great,

will take the case."

I knew what Oliver's

octopus looked like.

It had eight long, curling arms.

It looked oozy and slimy.

"Where do you keep
your octopus?" I asked.

"On my bookcase," Oliver said.

"But when I went to get it
this morning, it wasn't there."

"We must go to your house," I said.

I wrote a note to my mother.

I left the note at my house.

Then Sludge, Oliver, and I

went to Oliver's house.

He lives next door.

He took us to his room.

I saw his bookcase.

It was full of books.

So far, so good.

But it was squeezed

in a corner between the wall

and a huge tank of eels.

And the top of it was a mess.

It was covered

with baseball things.

Cards, gloves, balls, and bats.

"I've got so much stuff

on my bookcase
that some of it falls
to the floor,"
Oliver said.
"But I pick it right up."
"This is a real mess," I said.

"Your octopus must
be hidden under something
on top of your bookcase."
I, Nate the Great,
moved things,
piled things,
and sorted things.
Sludge sniffed.
"I have just found
something important," I said.
"What?" Oliver asked.
"A telephone. It was hidden
under two baseball gloves.
And the cord is still hidden."
"The cord goes down the back
of the bookcase

and plugs into the wall,"
Oliver said.

"It's boring.
But the telephone is nice.
I like to call people."

"I know it," I said.

Oliver is a pest.
He follows people.
He calls people.

At last I said,

"I do not see the octopus

on your bookcase."

"So you can't find it either,"

Oliver said.

"*On* is only one place to look,"

I said. "*In* is another."

I looked in Oliver's eel tank.

"Your octopus did not fall

in there," I said.

"Perhaps it fell

down one side

of your bookcase."

"But my bookcase

is squeezed between

the eel tank on one side

and the wall on the other,"
Oliver said.
"I, Nate the Great,
need a flashlight."
Oliver gave me a flashlight.
I flashed the light down

both sides of the bookcase.

"The octopus did not slip through,"

I said.

"So you struck out," Oliver said.

"No. There is one more place

to look. Perhaps your octopus

fell down the *back*

of the bookcase."

"But you can't get

back there,"

Oliver said.

"No problem. I, Nate the Great,

can peer over the top."

I leaned forward.

"Ouch!"

I bumped my head.

"The wall is in the way,"
I said. "I can't see down."
I stretched out flat
on the floor
in front of the bookcase.
"Now what are you doing?"
Oliver asked.
"I am flashing the flashlight
toward the floor at the back
of your bookcase," I said.
I, Nate the Great,
saw something.

I reached for it

and pulled it out.

It was not the octopus.

It was a baseball card.

"So *that's* where my

Babe Ruth card went!"

Oliver said.

"I, Nate the Great, say

that your octopus did not fall

down the back of your bookcase."

I walked around the room.

I looked hard.

"I do not see the octopus
anywhere in this room,"
I said. "When was the last time
you saw it?"

Oliver shrugged. "I'm not sure.
When I got home
from the game yesterday,
I pulled it out
of my pocket
and dumped it on my bookcase
with my other baseball stuff."

"Then what?"

"Then I used my telephone.
I called everybody I know."

"I believe it," I said.

"Then I went out and
followed people
for the rest of the day."

"I believe that too," I said.

"What did you do last night?"

"I slept," Oliver said.

I, Nate the Great,
was getting nowhere.

Oliver said, "This morning
when I went to get my octopus,
I couldn't find it."

"Has anyone else

been in this room?"

I asked.

"Only my eels," Oliver said.

"Then I, Nate the Great,

must go out and
look for clues."
"I will follow you,"
Oliver said.
"Stay by your telephone," I said.
Sludge and I went back
to the baseball field.
"The octopus was second base
in yesterday's game,"
I said to Sludge.

"Perhaps there's a clue here."
I saw Rosamond standing
under a tree with her cats.
"I just tossed my baseball mitt
into the air," she said.
"But it came down
on a branch of this tree
and it's stuck there."
I looked up.
I saw the mitt
on a branch.
"My cats can go up
and shake it down,"
Rosamond said.
"My cats are smart.
If Oliver's octopus

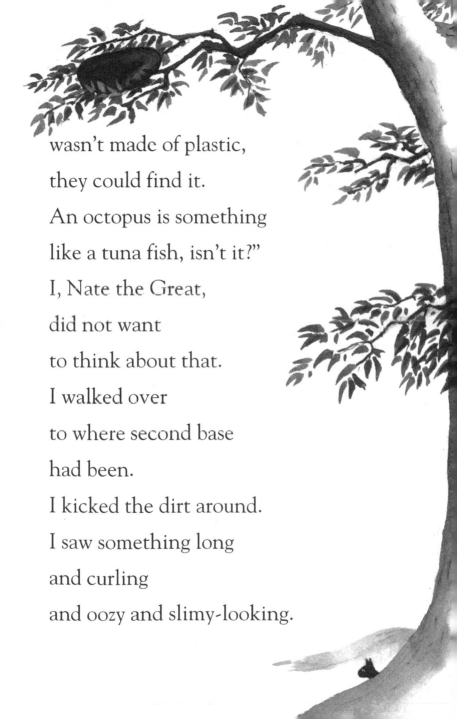

wasn't made of plastic,
they could find it.
An octopus is something
like a tuna fish, isn't it?"
I, Nate the Great,
did not want
to think about that.
I walked over
to where second base
had been.
I kicked the dirt around.
I saw something long
and curling
and oozy and slimy-looking.

It was one arm of Oliver's
octopus.
Oliver's octopus had eight arms.
I had found one.
I had solved one eighth
of this case.
"Look for more octopus arms,"
I said to Sludge.
Sludge and I walked
around the field.
The Sludge ran ahead.
He sniffed.
He stopped.

He brought me another octopus arm.

"Good work, Sludge," I said.

We kept looking.

But we could not find

any more octopus arms.

Sludge and I went home.

We had to think about the case.

I made pancakes for myself.

I gave Sludge a bone.

"We are looking for
a purple plastic octopus
with six arms,"
I said. "Or maybe less.
When Oliver took
the octopus home
from the last game,
he dumped everything
on his bookcase.
He did not notice that

two arms were missing.

What else didn't he notice?"

I went to the telephone.

I called Oliver.

He answered right away.

"Who did you follow

before you went home

from yesterday's game?" I asked.

"Annie," he said.

"And your octopus was in

your pocket, right?"

"Right," Oliver said.

"Thank you," I said.

I hung up.

"We must go to Annie's house,"

I said to Sludge.

Annie was sitting in front
with Fang.
"I am looking for
octopus arms," I said.
I looked at Fang.
I did not want to do that.
"Your dog will eat almost anything,"
I said. "Like second base."

"Why would he eat
gloopy purple plastic?" Annie said.
She held up a dog bone.
"This is third base
and Fang didn't eat it.
I'm very proud of him."
Fang wagged his tail.
"But Fang isn't perfect,"
Annie said.
That was no surprise to me,
Nate the Great.
Fang stopped wagging.
Annie said, "When Oliver
followed me after the last game,
Fang followed Oliver.
I think Fang snatched

some of the octopus

from Oliver's pocket."

"Aha!" I said. "So second base

was stolen after all."

"Fang only took

one octopus arm,"

Annie said. "And here it is."

Annie handed a very dirty

octopus arm to me.

"I just found this

in my yard," she said.

"Fang buried it there."

"Did Oliver see the snatch?"

I asked.

"No," Annie said.

"He was too busy following me."

"So Oliver's octopus
is missing three arms
and maybe more,
and Oliver doesn't know it,"
I said.
I said good-bye to Annie.
"This case is as good as solved,"
I said to Sludge.
"All we need to find
are a few more octopus arms."
We went to Oliver's house.
Oliver was talking
on the telephone.

Oliver kept talking.

I knew what I must do:

Get down on the floor.

Reach under the bookcase.

And unplug the telephone

from the wall.

But when I had looked

under there for the octopus,

I did not see the plug

or the cord.

They must have been

too high up.

I had to think of something else.

"HANG UP!" I shouted.

It worked.

Oliver hung up.

I held up the three octopus arms.

"I, Nate the Great, found these.

The case is in good shape.

But your octopus is not."

"I know that," Oliver said.

"When I brought it home,

I saw that I had

a five-armed octopus

instead of one with eight arms."

"Why didn't you tell me?"

I asked.

Oliver smiled.

"What difference does that make

to an octopus?

Five are plenty."

It made a big difference

to me, Nate the Great.

I said, "Then I still have to find

a mostly together octopus."

"Right," Oliver said.

I said, "I, Nate the Great,

have struck out.

But I will be back."

Sludge and I went

to the field.

Rosamond and her cats

were gone.

Her mitt was gone

from the tree.

I sat down on a log.

Sludge sat beside me.

I thought about the case.

I had found a telephone,

a baseball card,

and octopus arms.

None of these mattered.

Or did they?

I looked up at the tree

where Rosamond's mitt

had been stuck.

Hmmm.

I thought about the telephone again.

And the octopus arms.

Those *long, curling* arms.

And I knew where the octopus

had to be!

Sludge and I ran back
to Oliver's house.
Oliver was talking
on the telephone.
I started to pull his bookcase
away from the wall.
Oliver hung up.
"I need to look

43

behind your bookcase," I said.

I, Nate the Great, pulled harder.

Then I peered behind the bookcase.

I saw the telephone cord

plugged into the wall.

And I saw something else.

Stuck on the cord,

with two of its arms

curled around it,

was a five-armed

purple plastic octopus.

The case was solved!

I reached in to grab the octopus.

R-I-P!

The octopus now had four arms.

But that was plenty.

I held up the octopus.

"You found second base!"

Oliver said. "But how

did you know it was there?"

"Your octopus's arms are long

and curling," I said.

"That makes it easy

for them to catch

onto something.

That was a clue.

But I didn't know it
until I thought
about Rosamond's mitt
that had caught
on a branch.
It fell there
after she tossed it.
It should have landed
on the ground.
When your octopus
fell off the back

of your bookcase,

it should have landed

on the floor.

That's where I looked.

But it never got there.

Because its arms were caught

on the telephone cord."

"Hooray!" Oliver said. "Now we

can have baseball practice.

I will call the team."

Oliver made his calls

while I pushed the bookcase back.

Then Oliver, Sludge, and I

walked to the field.

I, Nate the Great,

went up to bat.

I looked around the field.

I saw first base.

A tuna fish can.

I saw second base.

Oliver's four-armed octopus.

Then I saw third base.

The dog bone was there.

In Fang's teeth.

Fang was third base.

I gripped the bat.

I, Nate the Great, hoped

I would strike out.

~Extra~
Fun Activities!

What's Inside

NATE'S NOTES:
The All-American Game

In 2005, more than 73 million fans went to pro baseball games.

In 2005, about two million American kids played Little League ball.

America is the birthplace of baseball! The first amateur teams formed in the early 1800s. Everyone played by slightly different rules.

Alexander Joy Cartwright invented modern baseball. He wrote down the rules in 1845.

The Cincinnati Red Stockings became the first pro team in 1869.

Baseball is popular outside America too. The game is especially big in Japan. PURE BORU! (That's Japanese for "Play ball!")

5

NATE'S NOTES: Great Players

These baseball players are some of the all-time greats. Who is your favorite?

NOLAN RYAN had the longest career in baseball. He played for 27 years.

MICKEY MANTLE hit the longest home run ever. He whacked the ball 634 feet in 1960.

634

TY COBB holds the record for the highest career batting average.

HANK AARON hit 755 home runs during his career. That's more than any other major-league player in history.

LOU GEHRIG hit 23 grand slams. A grand slam is a home-run hit with runners on first, second, and third bases.

KEN GRIFFEY SENIOR and his son KEN GRIFFEY JUNIOR played for the Seattle Mariners at the same time. During one game, they hit back-to-back home runs.

DEION SANDERS played in both baseball's World Series and football's Super Bowl.

NATE'S NOTES: Octopuses

An octopus makes a weird base. Octopuses are also weird animals. Nate found these facts at the library:

An octopus has eight legs. Each one is covered in suction cups. Octopuses have no bones. They have no shells. Their birdlike beaks are their only hard part.

Octopuses are very good at defending themselves.

• They can squirt a cloud of thick black ink at predators. Now you see them, now—SQUIRT!— you don't.

• They are great at changing colors. They can hide by blending into the background. They can turn alarming colors to warn off big hungry fish.

• A few octopus species can pretend to be more dangerous fish. They mimic eels. They act like lionfish. Some octopuses creep along the ocean floor pretending to be coconuts. Nutty!

The smallest octopus is the California octopus. Adults are just an inch long.

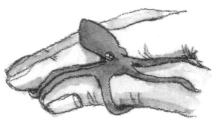

The largest? The North Pacific octopus. They can grow to 30 feet long and weigh 100 pounds.

Octopuses are smart! They can open jars.

Some even escape their aquariums to search for snacks. (They like crabs.)

STRANGE BUT TRUE:
Adult female North Pacific octopuses have exactly 2,240 suckers. That's 280 on each arm.

How to Make Octopus Pops

These pops will cool you off after an afternoon in the outfield. They look like octopuses.

GET TOGETHER:

- 6 small Dixie cups (3-ounce size)
- 2 cups of fruit juice (Any kind will work. Pink or purple juice makes the pops look more octopus-y.)
- 6 craft sticks
- 48 gummy worms (Again, pink or purple ones are best.)

MAKE YOUR OCTOPUS POPS:

1. Pour ⅓ cup of juice into each cup. Each one should be about ¾ full.
2. Put 8 gummy worms in each cup, lining them up around the edges. These are your octopus's legs.
3. Place the cups in the freezer for a few hours.
4. Place a stick in the center of each cup.
5. Return the cups to the freezer. Leave them there overnight.
6. Peel off the cups.
7. Eat your octopus pops!

Funny Pages

Q: Why did the baseball player go to jail?
A: He tried to steal second base.

Q: Why does it get hot after a baseball game?
A: All the fans leave.

Q: What runs around a baseball field but never scores?
A: A fence.

Q: Why didn't Cinderella make
   the baseball team?
A: She ran away
   from the
   ball.

Q: How is a baseball game like a pancake?
A: They both depend on the batter.

Q: What do you call a
   baseball covered
   in bugs?
A: A fly ball.

Q: What did the girl octopus say to the boy octopus?

A: I want to hold your hand, hand, hand, hand, hand, hand, hand, hand.

Q: How does an octopus go into battle?

A: Fully armed.

Q: What do you get if you cross a cow and an
   octopus?
A: A critter that can milk itself.

TV Newscaster: "Eight diamond watches
were stolen from a jeweler downtown. Police
are looking for a punctual octopus."

Doctor, Doctor, I think I'm an octopus.
*I'm sorry, but I can't examine you through this
cloud of ink.*

30 Teams, 30 Facts

The **Los Angeles Angels**
actually play in Anaheim,
the home of Disneyland.

Disneyland

President George W. Bush used to own the
Texas Rangers.

In 1989, the **San Francisco Giants** faced the
Oakland A's in the World Series. Play was
delayed for 10 days after a strong earthquake hit
San Francisco.

The **Dodgers** moved
from Brooklyn, New York,
to Los Angeles in 1958.

Another team's coach
once called the **Oakland
Athletics** white elephants.
He meant it as an insult.
But now a white elephant
is the team symbol.

The **Seattle Mariners** play at Safeco Field. The stadium cost $517 million to build. It's the most expensive ballpark in Major League Baseball.

For one game each year, the **Chicago White Sox** let fans bring their dogs to the ballpark.

In 1920, a pitch hit the **Cleveland Indians'** Ray Chapman in the head. He died the next day. Chapman is the only player who has died from a game-related injury. Batting helmets help protect players today.

The **Boston Red Sox** went 86 years between World Series wins. Some fans believed that Babe Ruth, who was traded from the Red Sox to the Yankees in 1920, cursed the team.

The **Kansas City Royals** played their first game in 1969. Just three years later, they finished second in the league.

The **Minnesota Twins** won their first World Series in 1987.

In 2002, the **Detroit Tigers** hosted an octopus-throwing contest.

In 1970, the **Baltimore Orioles** finished 15 games in front of the second-place New York Yankees. The Orioles went on to win the World Series.

The **Tampa Bay Devil Rays** play at Tropicana Field. The field was built to attract a team to Florida. It took eight years before the Devil Rays came.

The **New York Yankees** have won a record 26 World Series.

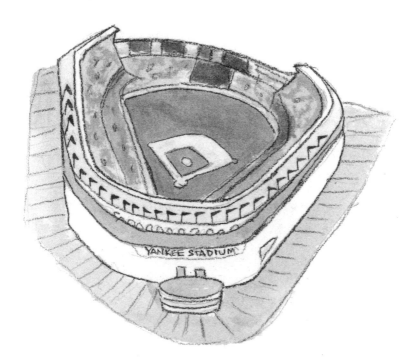

The **Toronto Blue Jays** are the only major-league team based in Canada.

In 2001, the **Arizona Diamondbacks** won the World Series. The team was only four years old.

The **Colorado Rockies** are famous for their hitting records. One reason? They play in Denver's mountains. The thin air helps the ball travel farther.

No **San Diego Padres** pitcher has ever pitched a no-hitter.

The **Chicago Cubs** haven't won a World Series since 1908.

In 1935, the **Cincinnati Reds** hosted the first major-league night game.

In 1997, the **Milwaukee Brewers** changed leagues. They moved from the American League to the National League.

AstroTurf is named after the **Houston Astros**. The plastic grass was first used in the team's stadium, the Astrodome, in 1966. Real grass wouldn't grow there.

In 1903, the **Pittsburgh Pirates** lost the first World Series ever played. Boston won.

The **Atlanta Braves** won 11 division championships in a row from 1995 to 2005.

In 1993, the **Florida Marlins** finished in sixth place in their league. They finished fifth in 1994. They finished fourth in 1995 and third in 1996. In 1997, they finished second and went on to win the World Series.

Cardinals fans are supposed to be baseball's best. That's why **St. Louis** is nicknamed Baseball City, U.S.A.

The **New York Mets** were the first team to host an official Banner Day. LET'S GO, METS!

Before 2005, the **Washington Nationals** played in Montreal. They were called the Expos.

In August 1922, the Chicago Cubs beat the **Philadelphia Phillies** 26 to 23. The 49-run score is an all-time game high.

How to Make Caramel Corn

Caramel corn is a great baseball snack. It's nice to eat if you're watching the game on TV.

Ask an adult to help with this recipe.

GET TOGETHER:

- 4 cups of freshly popped corn
- salt
- a shallow roasting pan
- a heavy saucepan
- 1 cup of brown sugar
- ⅓ cup (1 stick) of butter
- ½ cup of light corn syrup
- ½ teaspoon of vanilla
- ½ teaspoon of baking soda

MAKE YOUR CARAMEL CORN:

1. Preheat the oven to 250 degrees.
2. Lightly salt the popcorn.
3. Place the popcorn in the roasting pan.
4. In the saucepan, mix the sugar, butter, and corn syrup. Get your adult helper to stir the mixture over medium heat until it boils.
5. Boil the mixture for five minutes without stirring.

6. Remove the saucepan from the heat. Stir in the vanilla and baking soda.
7. Pour the mixture over the popcorn. Stir to coat well.
8. Bake for one hour.
9. Cool. Break into small clumps.
10. Eat while cheering on your favorite team!

Have you helped solve all Nate the Great's mysteries?

❑ **Nate the Great and the Snowy Trail**: Nate has his work cut out for him when his friend Rosamond loses the birthday present she was going to give him. How can he find the present when Rosamond won't even tell him what it is?

❑ **Nate the Great and the Fishy Prize**: The trophy for the Smartest Pet Contest has disappeared! Will Sludge, Nate's clue-sniffing dog, help solve the case and prove he's worthy of the prize?

❑ **Nate the Great Stalks Stupidweed**: When his friend Oliver loses his special plant, Nate searches high and low. Who knew a little weed could be so tricky?

❑ **Nate the Great and the Boring Beach Bag**: It's no relaxing day at the beach for Nate and his trusty dog, Sludge, as they search through sand and surf for signs of a missing beach bag.

❑ **Nate the Great Goes Down in the Dumps**: Nate discovers that the only way to clean up this case is to visit the town dump. Detective work can sure get dirty!

❑ **Nate the Great and the Halloween Hunt**: It's Halloween, but Nate isn't trick-or-treating for candy. Can any of the witches, pirates, and robots he meets help him find a missing cat?

❑ **Nate the Great and the Musical Note**: Nate is used to looking for clues, not listening for them! When he gets caught in the middle of a musical riddle, can he hear his way out?

- **Nate the Great and the Stolen Base**: It's not easy to track down a stolen base, and Nate's hunt leads him to some strange places before he finds himself at bat once more.

- **Nate the Great and the Pillowcase**: When a pillowcase goes missing, Nate must venture into the dead of night to search for clues. Everyone sleeps easier knowing Nate the Great is on the case!

- **Nate the Great and the Mushy Valentine**: Nate hates mushy stuff. But when someone leaves a big heart taped to Sludge's doghouse, Nate must help his favorite pooch discover his secret admirer.

- **Nate the Great and the Tardy Tortoise**: Where did the mysterious green tortoise in Nate's yard come from? Nate needs all his patience to follow this slow . . . slow . . . clue.

- **Nate the Great and the Crunchy Christmas**: It's Christmas, and Fang, Annie's scary dog, is not feeling jolly. Can Nate find Fang's crunchy Christmas mail before Fang crunches on *him*?

- **Nate the Great Saves the King of Sweden**: Can Nate solve his *first-ever* international case without leaving his own neighborhood?

- **Nate the Great and Me: The Case of the Fleeing Fang**: A surprise Happy Detective Day party is great fun for Nate until his friend's dog disappears! Help Nate track down the missing pooch, and learn all the tricks of the trade in a special fun section for aspiring detectives.

❑ **Nate the Great and the Monster Mess**: Nate loves his mother's deliciously spooky Monster Cookies, but the recipe has vanished! This is one case Nate and his growling stomach can't afford to lose.

❑ **Nate the Great, San Francisco Detective**: Nate visits his cousin Olivia Sharp in the big city, but it's no vacation. Can he find a lost joke book in time to save the world?

❑ **Nate the Great and the Big Sniff**: Nate depends on his dog, Sludge, to help him solve all his cases. But Nate is on his own this time, because Sludge has disappeared! Can Nate solve the case and recover his canine buddy?

❑ **Nate the Great on the Owl Express**: Nate boards a train to guard Hoot, his cousin Olivia Sharp's pet owl. Then Hoot vanishes! Can Nate find out *whooo* took the feathered creature?